First published in the United States in 2009 by Prinny Books, an imprint of NIS America, Inc.
English translation © 2009 by NIS America, Inc.
Localized by Hiroko Kanazashi, Steven Carlton, Yoko Nishikawa

Copyright © 2008 Mayumi Ichikawa and Takashi Yamamoto
English letters presented in pictures are not by the original illustrator.
Originally published by BRONZE PUBLISHING Inc., Tokyo, Japan, in
2008 under the title of "Ninja Tsubamemaru".
The English rights arranged with BRONZE PUBLISHING Inc., Tokyo.
All rights reserved.
Manufactured in Singapore.

Library of Congress Control Number: 2009928877
ISBN-13: 978-0-9824411-2-1
ISBN-10: 0-9824411-2-6

NIS America, Inc.
1221 E. Dyer. Rd., Suite 210, Santa Ana, CA 92705, USA

Tsubame the Ninja

Author: Mayumi Ichikawa   Illustrator: Takashi Yamamoto

In one small ordinary town, there is one ordinary house.

Prinny Books

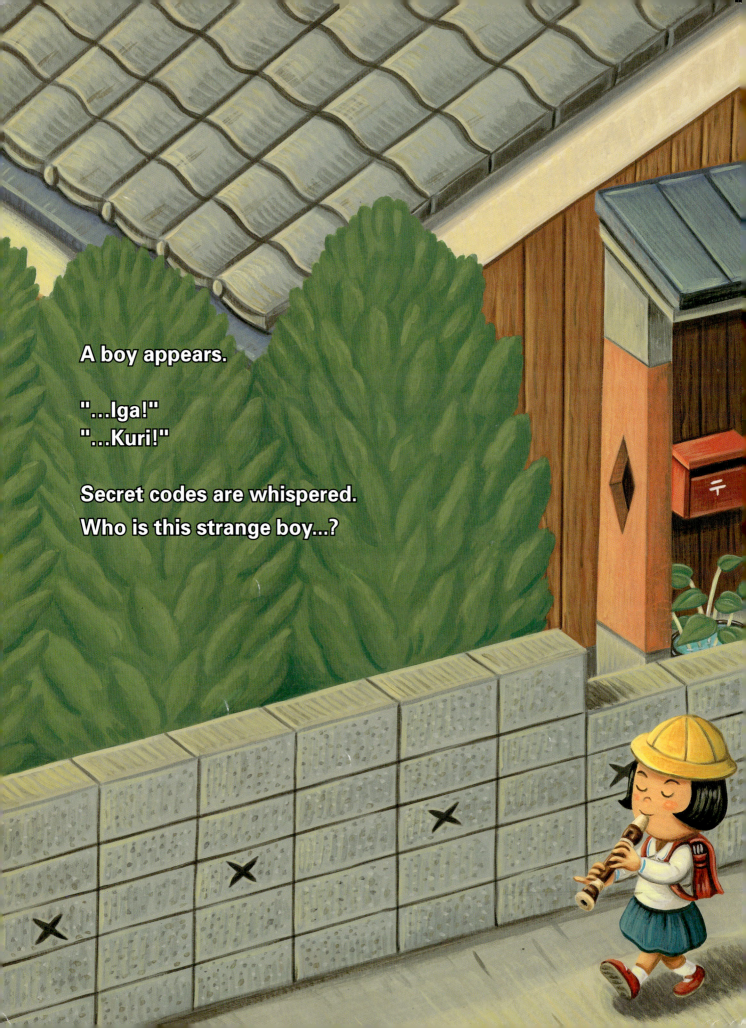

A boy appears.

"...Iga!"
"...Kuri!"

Secret codes are whispered.
Who is this strange boy...?

"I'm home!"
Tsubame is his name.
On his shoulder is Hayate the swallow.

"Welcome home, big brother!"
Welcoming him are his little brothers,
Karasu and Kokamo.

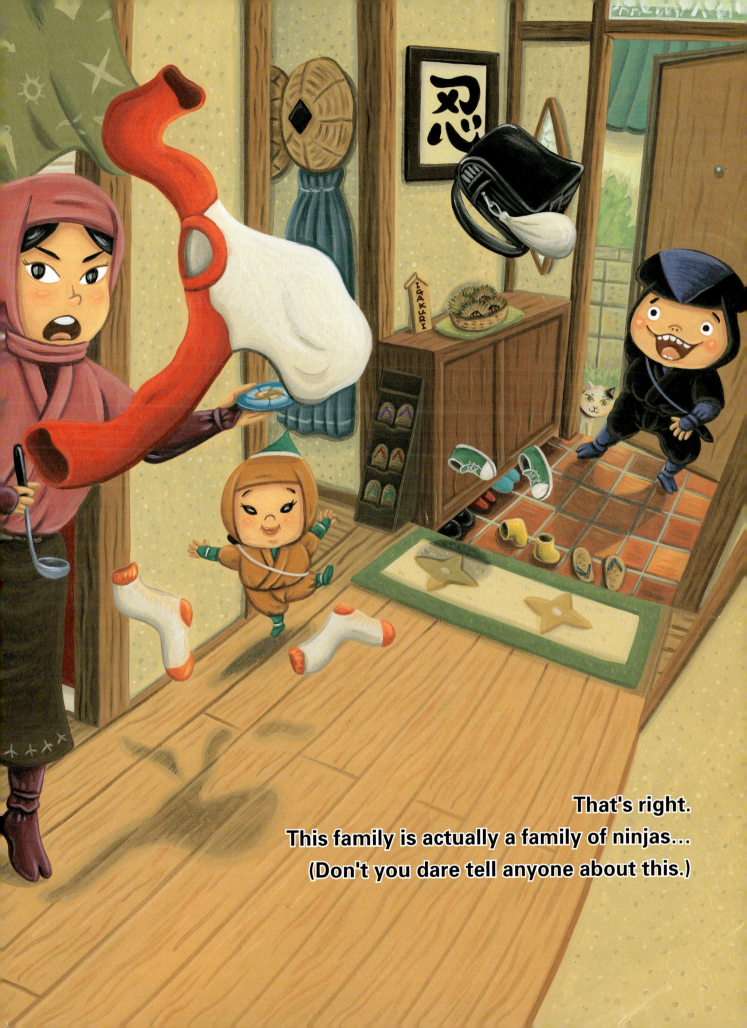

That's right.
This family is actually a family of ninjas…
(Don't you dare tell anyone about this.)

Ninja Time begins at night.
Once the sun sets,
it is time to train!

"Tahhh!"
"Urahh!"

First comes "Target Practice with Ninja Stars"...

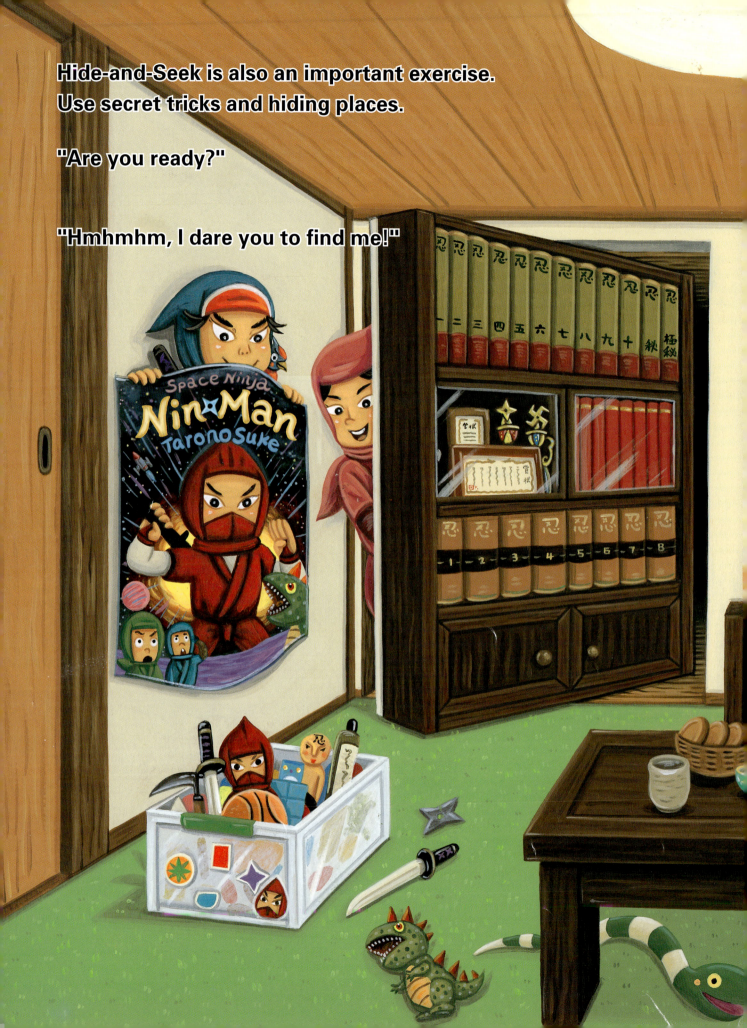

But listen to this.
Tsubame just can't master the skill of "Jiori",
where he has to use his ninja jacket to glide down.
He gets too nervous once he looks down from great heights and it makes him almost pee his pants!

"Oh so you can't jump, big brother?"

He can't even say a word,
even when his brothers make fun of him.

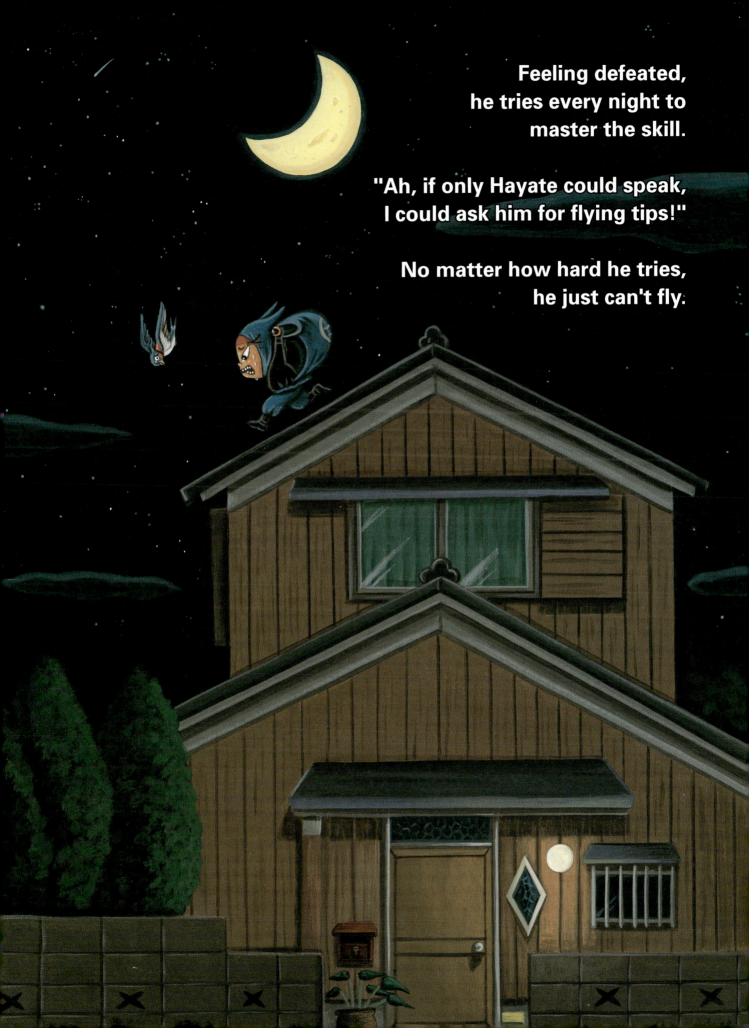

On the night of the full moon, peeking out between the clouds...

Oh? How unusual.
Where is the whole family going?
Sprinting for a great distance.
"Tonight is going to be great!"

Hmm, where is this...?

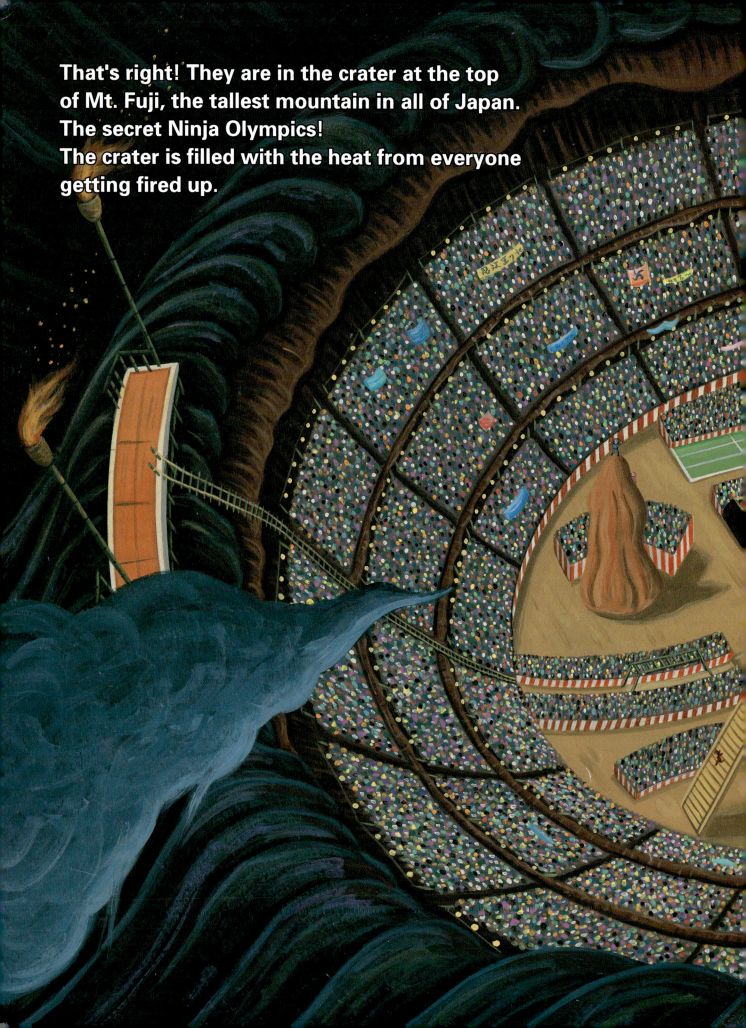

That's right! They are in the crater at the top of Mt. Fuji, the tallest mountain in all of Japan. The secret Ninja Olympics!
The crater is filled with the heat from everyone getting fired up.

"Suiton" (Bamboo Snorkel), "Bunshin" (Mirror Images), and "Mekuramashi" (Blinding Flash). Tsubame's family is very excited about the fierce battles! Now, it's time for the night's main event! Uh oh, where is Tsubame?

Oh look, there he is!
He is mumbling a chant to calm his mind.
"Rin, Hyo, To, Sha, Kai, Jin, Retsu, Zai, Zen"
It's a victory chant, making symbolic signs with his fingers.

"Tsubame, I will beat you! Croak!"
The excited one is Tsubame's rival, Gama.
The "Ninja Obstacle Course" is starting.
Tsubame trained very hard for tonight.
Finally, it's Tsubame's turn!

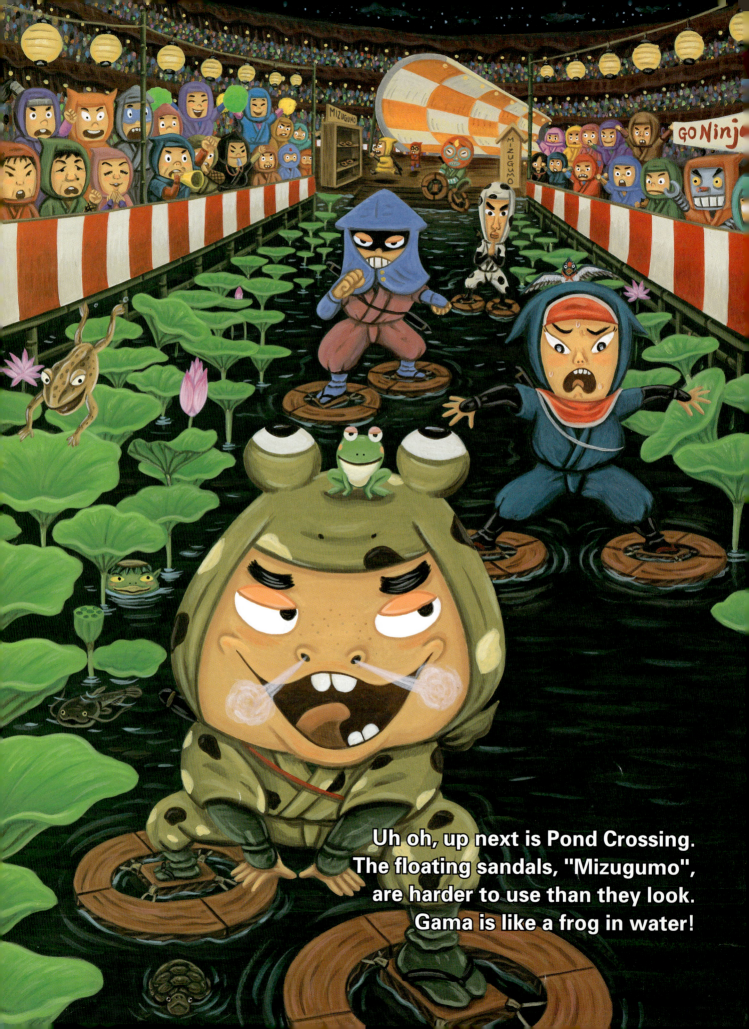

With Makibishi spikes spread all over the ground, fly over them using the "Hook Rope". Tsubame takes the lead again!

Now he's close to the finish line!
The last course is actually Tsubame's
least favorite, the "Jiori Glider" !!!
It's a challenging skill,
jumping off the rim of the crater.

"Alright, I can do this. I can jump,
I can, I can, I know I can!
I think I can... Can I really? ...
Oh boy, I can't do this!"

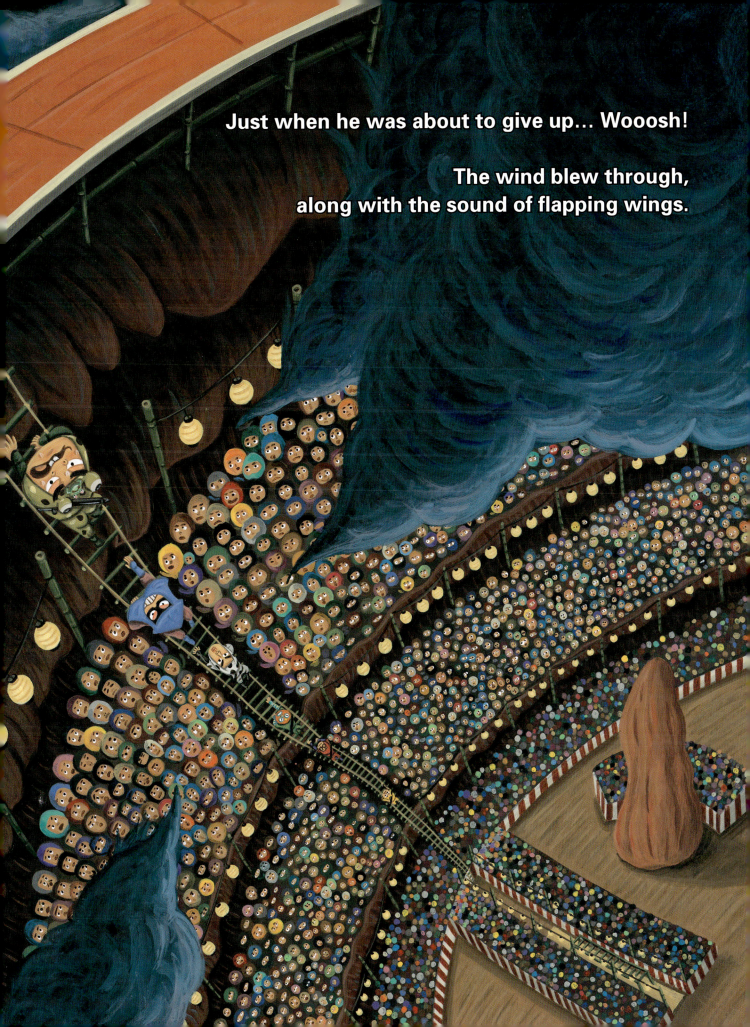

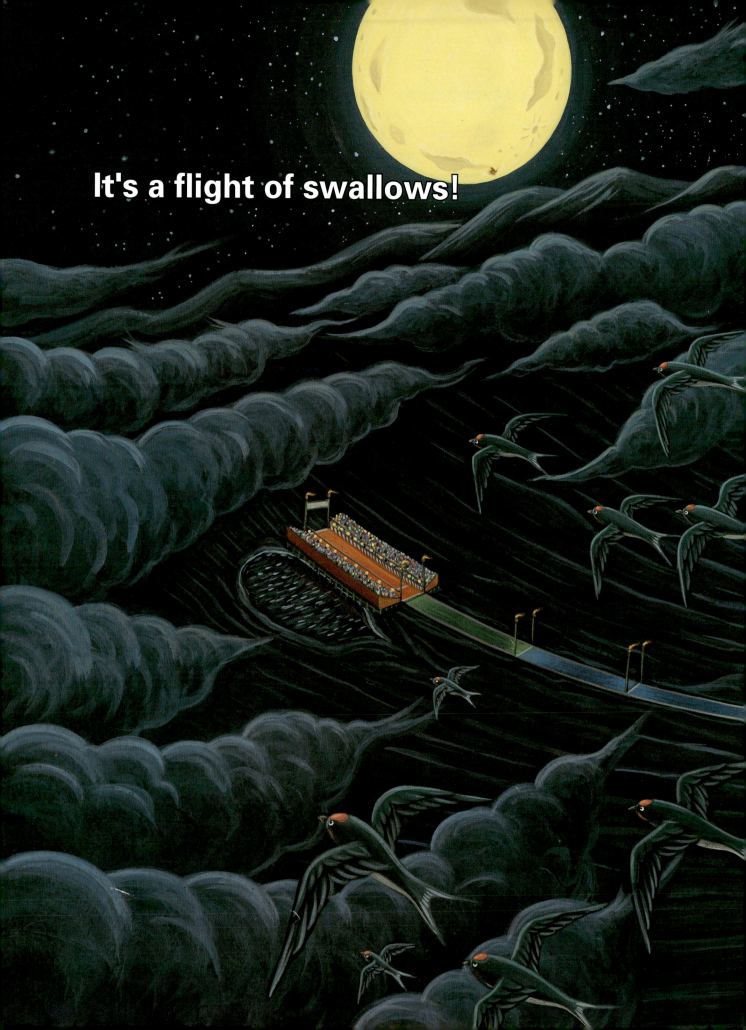

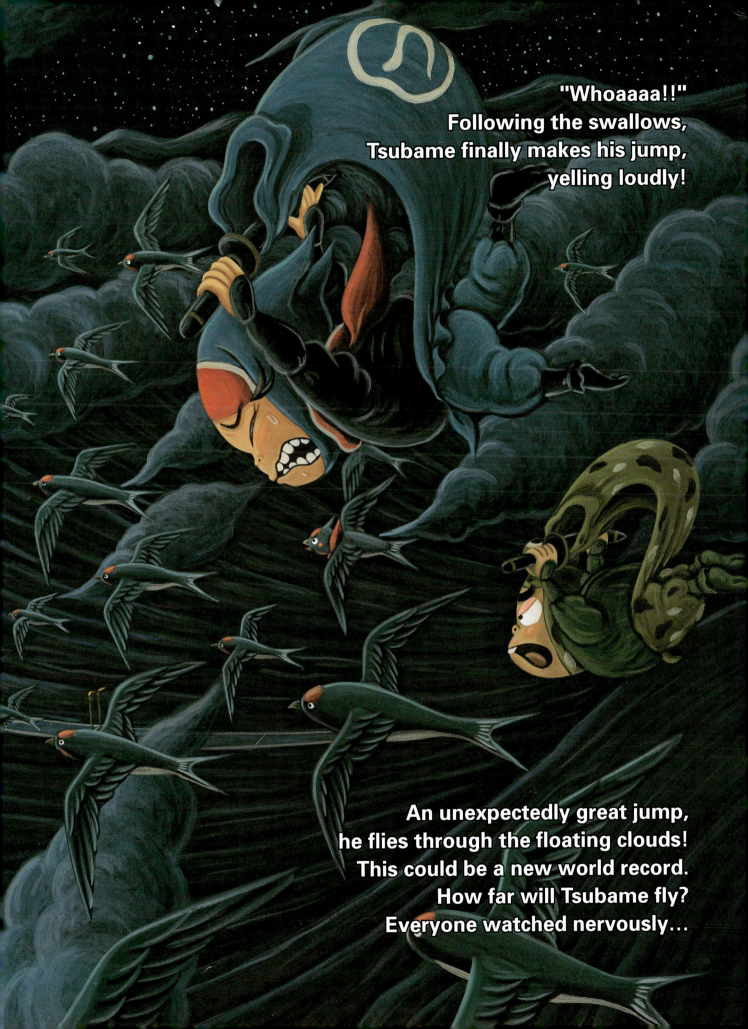

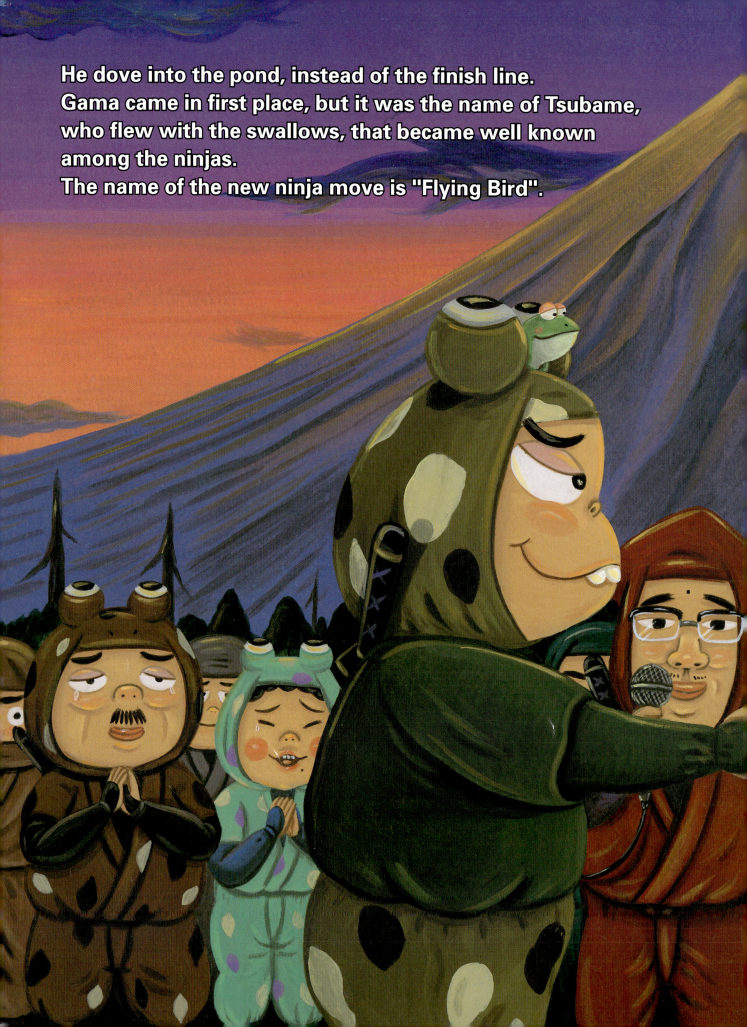

He dove into the pond, instead of the finish line.
Gama came in first place, but it was the name of Tsubame, who flew with the swallows, that became well known among the ninjas.
The name of the new ninja move is "Flying Bird".

It's almost time for sunrise.
After saying their goodbyes, all of the ninjas changed into their daytime disguises and scattered to the North and South.
It's about time to say goodbye here, Ninja Vanish!

Author: Mayumi Ichikawa

Born in Kanagawa, 1974.
Ichikawa started making stories while working
full-time at a company.
Tsubame the Ninja is her first picture book.
Ichikawa loves traveling and belly dancing. She is interested in
Asian history and languages.

Illustrator: Takashi Yamamoto

Born in Ehime, 1972.
Yamamoto graduated from Osaka Designer's College with a
picture book art major. He lives in a town near the sea with his
wife, who is also a picture book author.